THE PINK INSTITUTION

The Pink Institution

A NOVEL BY

Selah Saterstrom

COFFEE HOUSE PRESS

2004

Coffee House Press books are available to the trade through our primary distributor, Consortium Book Sales & Distribution, 1045 Westgate Drive, Saint Paul, MN 55114. For personal orders, catalogs, or other information, write to: Coffee House Press, 27 North Fourth Street, Suite 400, Minneapolis, MN 55401.

Coffee House Press is a nonprofit literary publishing house. Support from private foundations, corporate giving programs, government programs, and generous individuals help make the publication of our books possible. We gratefully acknowledge their support in detail in the back of this book.

To you and our many readers around the world,
we send our thanks for your continuing support.

LIBRARY OF CONGRESS CIP INFORMATION

Saterstrom, Selah, 1974–
The pink institution : a novel / by Selah Saterstrom.
p. cm.
ISBN 1-56689-155-8 (alk. paper)
1. Women—Mississippi—Fiction. 2. Mothers and daughters—Fiction.
3. Mississippi—Fiction. I. Title.
PS3619.A818P56 2004
813'.6—DC22

FIRST EDITION

3   5   7   9   10   8   6   4   2

PRINTED IN CANADA

~~~~~~~~

ACKNOWLEDGMENTS

Portions of this book have appeared in:
3rd Bed, Tarpaulin Sky, Monkey Puzzle, Web Conjunctions,
and *Experimental Theology,* published by the Seattle Research Institute.

I am indebted to Penny Murphy, Helen Green, and Katherine Babin.
Thank you for everything.

10% of author proceeds go to The Sunshine Shelter For Abused and Neglected Children in Natchez, Mississippi, in support of the pioneering efforts of Gail Healy.

To them, and to NS, RB, MK, and JM, my deepest thanks.

For my parents,
and in memory of my grandmothers.

Contents

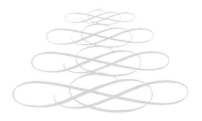

*B*EAUTIFUL WOMEN HERE *Cheek char it. Pink aplatter her and her and her. Beautiful Women Are Haunted Houses. Watching I each. Troughing watch. Othered. You watching you watch. "Extraordinary; remarkable." Sister, can I get-ah. Red and white striped, take for starvations. Discounted two by two by two. Women and children first.*

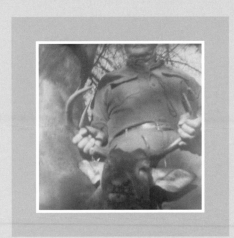

i

"The day the war began
is known as Ruination Day"

The following tableaux tell the true story of a young man [text smear   ] The reverence with which the [text smear   ]people take part in their tableaux at once captures the imagination of the spectators and [text smear   ] truly "live in the past" with Beau Repose. The Confederate Ball so [text smear   ] the days of the old South that it has become likened to the [text smear   ] Passion [text smear   ] and has become famous as the old houses.

THE CONFEDERATE BALL
PROGRAM GUIDE, 1938

The   mother   watched

how   each   day   after   school

the   child   broke   the   cracker

into   equally   sized   sections   then

one   at   a   time

put   the   sections

into   her   mouth

by   pushing   them   to   the   back

of   her   tongue   each   time

all   five   fingers

entered   her   mouth.

The   mother   said,

looks   like   a   rat   nest   that   hair

a   nest   for   rats.

She careful put the cracker section she was holding back on the table top with her moist fingers she touched the ends of her hair.

"Tableau: Family Prayers"

Unlike many past civilizations which acquired tremendous wealth these people, although gay and admirers of the beautiful in all things [text smear] remained deeply religious. Daily prayers were said by the master of the plantation in which all the household reverently joined.

THE CONFEDERATE BALL
PROGRAM GUIDE, 1938

We   knew   it   began   with   a   mother
dropping   a   spoon   or   a   knife
it   began   pink   translucent   vein   slippered
wrapped in baby skin inside a mother a mother
lies   in   bed,   a   single   lamp   burns.
A   thin   water   red   over   a   sweaty   mother
is linen thread yanked through smell of boiled sheets.
A   mother   shits   the   bed   stomach   pounding
stuffed with too big a heart goes soft in the middle
and   it   comes.

A   man   enjoyed   hunting

a   woman   enjoyed

socializing and thinking about restoration projects to repair damage done from the Civil War. Abella gave birth.

Micajah was the law she lived in the town he lived in the country. Children lived between versions suggest the couple adored one another others that they detested.

The   family   would   have   Sunday   dinner

cooked   by   a   domestic   servant

the   servant's   name   was   Lacuna

a   Ladies'   Garden   Club,   a   loaded   rifle

cooked   by   a   black   woman

named   Lacuna   who   moved   in   with   him

versions   suggest   others

that   they   detested

Micajah

was   an   alcoholic

Abella   liked

sherry   and   always   kept

her   town   table   set.

Abella   wanted   only   beautiful   children.

Beautiful   children   had   curly   hair.

She   made   inquiries   and   learned

from   a   syphilis   half   blind   back

country   bastard   child   deliverer

if she shaved the children's heads and soaked them in sugarwater the hair would grow back curly. When the children got lice, Abella seized her opportunity She shaved the heads and soaked the heads in   sugarwater   sugarwater   is piss   slang. The children's hair grew back but straight save one named Azalea   grew   ring   lets.

Abella and Micajah departed for an evening departed of the country while the children seated in the kitchen ate. That day the ceilings had been puttied with thick plaster. Departing Micajah turned, said whatever you do don't throw your dinner into that ceiling once departed with excitement children began to throw peas into that ceiling but not Azalea Micajah asked which had done what he said not to do they pointed to Azalea she received the strap the peas remained she did not did so did not he her undeparted.

"Tableau:
Falling in Love"

In this lovely setting the Northerner finds
the one girl of his [text smear   ] dreams.
This completes the happiness he has found
in the easy, peaceful life of the South and he
decides to remain and seek his fortune in
this rich land of cotton plantations.

THE CONFEDERATE BALL
PROGRAM GUIDE, 1938

Willie's father was a merchant with tailored white linen suits with impeccable posture from Boston young, he decided to reincorporate the South into the blood he married Willie's mother Willie's mother from Mississippi hated Boston she hated blood the line he hated reincorporated hate blooded it.

A Mr. Peters accepted a position at the Beau Repose Female Academy where he recognized writing talent in Azalea.

Azalea understood herself a romance writer, but not Mr. Peters. He said write simple narrative, something a twelve-year-old could understand.

Azalea was insulted nonetheless Mr. Peters negotiated a scholarship for her to study English at the University of the South.

On a Sunday afternoon it was with excitement, because Willie loved to sketch, with his artistic nature in mind, it was with excitement, Azalea told Willie on a Sunday afternoon something a twelve-year-old could understand.

He said No wife of mine is going to a college. The couple married. Willie drove Azalea to Boston for a honeymoon.

Two months after the day he left for North Africa to work as an attorney for the military during wartime, Azalea went to the doctor. She was pregnant.

Willie said he had known he would marry her, Since that day I saw you doing cartwheels in the lawn. On that day was her birthday, the day she turned twelve.

That day there was a thunderstorm. Azalea was walking under her umbrella down Main Street when a passing car came to a halt. It was Mr. Peters Mr. Peters who did not have an umbrella Mr. Peters standing by his car in the rain pointed to her extended belly, said, What the hell is that? Mr. Peters, don't you know? Mr. Peters shook his head simple narrative so a twelve-year-old could understand after which he got back in his car and resumed driving.

Azalea moved into the house
of Willie's mother .
found it so cruel she left and
moved into her father's house
where she spent the duration of the war.
Willie wrote to Azalea
they would have their own house
after the war. Word got round
that the first night of the Boston honeymoon
began in a New Orleans whorehouse.
Willie wrote to Azalea
we will have our own house
after war.

"Tableau:
The King and Queen
of Court"

A beautiful young girl is crowned Queen of the Ball.
She is accompanied by her maids who are met by
their escorts dressed in the uniforms of Confederate
Generals [text smear   ] They enter the hall
to the stirring sounds of Dixie.

THE CONFEDERATE BALL
PROGRAM GUIDE, 1938

After   the   war   Willie's   first   stop
was   to   his   mother's   house.
In   the   interim,   Azalea's   mother   Abella
learned of his return and requested he come for tea.
She   was   a   gracious   host   a
sterling tea service predating the Civil War she
placed one finger on the lid while guiding the slender
spout with another.

I do trust your journey home was a fine one

she said

Why it was

a fine one

he said

It sure is

a day

he said

Lovely

isn't it

you may have taken opportunity to smell my porch side

gardenias

she said

she said

I prefer the parlor to unbecoming places

don't you?

I could not agree with you

more

he said

In these modern times

any old street can be just such

an unbecoming place

she said

This can be true

he said

I think it is

I think it is true

she said

Well now   .

she said

might I inquire

just how

you find my parlor

is it acceptable?

Exceptional

he said

I rather think so

if I do say

being of this opinion

it should not surprise you

I think it better to hear

what your wife has been up to

in this fine parlor

than on the street.

When Willie arrived in the country Micajah and the toddler daughter whom he had never met greeted him. Azalea could not be found. When Willie found her the next morning she was crouched under a tree smelling of piss and gin.

A   gathering   at   the   Mississippi   River   levee
on a blanket by the river Azalea told Bootsy Johnson a
joke   and   after   Bootsy   Johnson   slapped   her   knee
while   Willie   watched   Willie   had   known
Bootsy   Johnson   all   of   his   life
Willie   picked   up   Bootsy   Johnson
began   to   punch   spleen   kidney
Willie   pointed   to   Azalea   doubled   over   yelled,
My   wife   is   a   whore.
Bootsy   Johnson   a   bloody   heap.

Azalea had slept with his friend but not one
from boyhood days for when Azalea was nine
cousin Jeremiah was considered good-natured
because   everyone   knew
he had drawn the short end of the stick
when Micajah took in the teenaged Jeremiah
everyone knew it was a Christian thing
Azalea   was   nine   when   Jeremiah
thereafter   raped   Azalea   she   knew
about   sex   before   marriage
from   his   friend   but   not   one
from   boyhood   days   for   Micajah
did   not   like   babies   but   Azalea
was   a   baby   he   liked.

By the time

she was a young girl his devotion

by the time she was prepubescent his devotion

by the time

she was a teenager

his devotion pearlesed.

Most people knew how Micajah was about Azalea.

Most people knew

how it was with them.

Willie and Azalea did not buy a house in the country but lived in a Victorian two-story on St. Clare Avenue owned by Willie's mother who would let herself in during night and wake Azalea demanding Azalea perform degrading chores how she would pull Azalea's hair. Willie and Azalea got onto the task of making a larger family. During her second pregnancy Mr. Peters's name caught Azalea's eye. She had not heard anything about Mr. Peters since the day in the rain. Reading the paper she learned he left Mississippi to move to of all places Central America the newspaper said Mr. Peters went into the jungle and shot himself in the head.

While living on St. Clare Avenue Azalea and Willie had two more children bringing the number to four. Faryn, Aza, Ginger, and Trulie. This did not include the son Willie had with a French woman during the war he said he saved her life and the only way she could repay him was with sex she was a lesbian before he saved her life he said but not after.

When   the   girls   got   new   shoes

Willie   would   call   them   into   the   kitchen

they would be ordered to remove the shoes from their feet

he would set each shiny patent pair on the table in

front   of   him   and   he   would   pull   out   his   knife

taking   each   in   turn

scoring   their   soles.

Once during the war Azalea sent Willie a photograph.

It was not Easter but she was wearing her Easter best.

It was an effort, for the war.

.

Micajah stood front and center surrounded by women.

Willie wrote back, You look wonderful, Darling. I can see

you've been reducing again. You mustn't Dear, it weakens.

You know I love you as is but Darling you do look

wonderful. Holding your photograph looking at Micajah,

how   jealous   I   feel.   He   must   be   a   king

to   have   such   an   attractive   harem.

ii

"*I can never recover my object*"

CHILDHOOD OBJECTS

Children's Room

Neighbors

Fire

Red Siren

Stationery

Doll

Crayon

Whistling

Spiderland

Hamper

Louisiana

There

Cissy's

Stampede

Children's Room

Willie lay in bed. Through darkness he made out a figure standing in the doorway. Willie realized it was Death. Death entered the room in long, swooping strides. He walked past Willie's bed and entered the adjoining children's room. Willie followed. Death picked up a child at which point Willie began to assault Death. The two entered a wrestling match. Willie won with child in arms and Death defeated, got up to leave, but he brought his mouth close and said, "You'll see me again." Death looked like the popular renderings.

～ Neighbors

Micajah made a loan to Azalea and Willie so they could buy a house adjacent to his property. The house was named Mary's Down. Built in the 1750s by the first Spanish governor of the Mississippi territory, it was in decline. Azalea, Willie, and the girls moved to Mary's Down. Other than Micajah, the nearest neighbors were Haggard and Dunbar Hyce. They had one son, Haggard, Jr. The Hyces moved to Toomsata plantation from Los Angeles, California. Dunbar's ancestors built Toomsata in the late 1700s. Because in years to follow her family left the South, they were not considered official Southerners. To make matters worse, they no longer maintained familial connections in Mississippi so the Hyces remained outside social acceptability. The Hyce family was brilliant. Haggard Hyce was a translator. His solitary project was translating the Bible into Chinese. He did upside down and backwards. He did not always answer to his name. Dunbar Hyce loved Toomsata. She would say its owner had returned and it would burn to the ground before it left the family again. Azalea and Willie began to socialize with the Hyces, but really with Dunbar. Dunbar was a small woman with dark eyes. Meanwhile, Azalea never showed the children affection and Willie was voted district judge by an overwhelming majority.

Fire

Often when Willie and Azalea would play cards and drink with Dunbar Hyce at Toomsata, they would leave the girls alone at Mary's Down. One such evening the girls were upstairs playing records when a fire broke out. The fire did not cause substantial damage. The next day when Willie and Azalea questioned the girls about the fire, they could not say. None had matches. Willie suggested a ghost started the fire. This seemed plausible and life resumed.

Red Siren

Faryn was Micajah's first grandchild. She loved his patrol car. Patrol cars had a single siren on top, activated by a small pedal on the floorboard inside the car. He would drive her through Lower Baton. Lower Baton was shotgun shacks, not covered by county sewage. He would put her between his legs on the floorboard. At the appropriate moment he would yell, "Make those niggers run!" Faryn would bear down with both hands on the pedal siren.

Stationery

Azalea discovered scratches on Ginger's face. Ginger said
two nuns had done it. Several days later Azalea went out
shopping. The old woman who watched the children saw
two nuns pulling Ginger toward the garden gate. She
began a child tug-of-war with the nuns. The nuns said
Ginger was a naughty child who escaped from the
orphanage. The old woman began praying in tongues.
haw   skimy   malahi   jeezzzuz   cr   eye   st.
The nuns ran away. Ginger acquired an expensive piece
of stationery on which she recorded the family's sins and
annoyed them all. There was no convent. There was in
1870, but it had burned.

Doll

Aza had red hair and green eyes. Willie, Azalea, and the other children had dark hair and brown eyes. One day Willie came home from work early. Azalea was in the kitchen making biscuits. Aza was playing dolls. She was sitting on the floor, leaning against the wall by the gas heater. Willie poured a drink. He said, "Well Azalea you can sigh a breath of relief. I had Aza's blood tested and she's mine." Aza's head fell back, hitting the wall, causing her long braids to fall into the grates of the gas heater. They went up in flames, then caught her whole head on fire. As Azalea hit her head to extinguish the fire, a layer of flour dust settled over the face of the child.

Crayon

Trulie, always small for her age, developed the habit of writing TRULIE WAS HERE with a crayon. She wrote this inside toilet rims, along baseboards, and under slats of beds. When asked why, she said it was because she was so small people might forget she was.

Whistling

After suffering two strokes, Willie's mother moved in. Before the strokes, she liked to dangle the children from windows. During occasional visits to her room, Aza, Ginger, and Trulie were afraid, but Faryn who had always adored her, found visits pleasant. Azalea never visited the room. Every day after work, Willie would enter the room and close the door. Exactly one hour later, he would reemerge. The old woman had insomnia. So bad some nights she would scream, but her screams sounded like whistles. Over time, the condition improved. She told the girls a fancy lady had begun to visit her at night. The fancy lady was beautiful. She had long hair and wore a hoop skirt with a wide blue satin sash. The fancy lady had a silver hairbrush. She would sit behind the old woman, brushing out the tangles of her matted hair. This made her sleep. The children asked if it could be true. Azalea said, "If it makes her stop that goddamned whining."

Eventually, an owl showed up on the porch, hooted three times, and the old woman died.

Spiderland

As soon as autumn arrived, after Sunday dinner Micajah would make the grandchildren get into the back of his pickup truck and he would drive them to Spiderland. On his property there was an old grove of trees. Every autumn large black spiders would nest, covering the trees in thick trampoline-like webbing. He would drive fast through the grove, destroying the webs and causing spiders to rain on the hysterical children. There were some accidents. Every Sunday the children would make him swear to God he would never take them to Spiderland again. Every Sunday he would swear not to. Other games with Micajah included the Passing Ice game in which he would put a piece of ice in his mouth and make the girls put their mouths to his and get it out.

Hamper

Willie and Azalea returned late from Toomsata to discover all the lights in the house off. The doors and windows were closed and locked. This was unusual. After breaking down two doors, Willie and Azalea found the girls hiding in the bathroom hamper closet, Aza holding a shotgun. Ginger had vomited. They said they were chased into the hamper closet by a hand banging that came from under the floors.

Louisiana

Travels included trips to Louisiana. Willie and Azalea intuited that Trulie had a problem with her legs so she was fitted for leg braces in Monroe. Every other Friday for several years, Willie, Azalea, and their nephew Stiney would drive Trulie to Monroe to have unnecessary doctor appointments. There were incidents involving motel rooms and police due to drinking. There were also spontaneous trips to New Orleans. Azalea would wake the children in the middle of the night and deposit them in the backseat of the car. They were told these New Orleans trips were for the sake of art.

⟨ There

Azalea sent Aza to Toomsata to see if Willie was there. Aza walked into the house. She asked Dunbar if her father was there. Dunbar said, "He's in the bed, you jealous little bitch." On several occasions the children watched Dunbar masturbate their drunk father while their mother, also drunk, slobbered on herself sitting in the corner.

Cissy's

Willie, the only judge to ever do so, shut down Cissy's, the local whorehouse, when a thirteen-year-old mulatto child was found dead. Several prominent men in the community held a private meeting with Willie, after which the whorehouse reopened.

Stampede

One night after the family had gone to bed there was a racket in the living room. It sounded like a stampede. After it subsided, Willie went into the living room. He said loudly, "I think y'all need to take a look at this." The family gathered in the living room. They saw what appeared to be muddy footprints of a large man going across the ceiling. It looked like the man had been running.

MAIDENHOOD OBJECTS

Dining Room

Willie called his daughters into the dining room. He picked up a dining room table chair and threw it into a closed window. The window shattered. He said, "That's a lesson about virginity. Do you understand?" to which they replied, "Yes sir."

~ *Chapel*

Toomsata had an underground chapel. One night Dunbar took the girls there. Inside were many coffins. Some of the coffin lids were partially off or caving in. There were a number of wooden coffins, nailed shut. Dunbar said, "See those nailed up ones? In the early 1800s pox raged through the territory and the living didn't know what to do. They didn't know what was causing the death. They figured the devil was though. A lot of people who lived in this house were sick. My ancestor, who owned this house, had those coffins built. He had servants bring the sick into this chapel and had them put in the coffins. They weren't dead yet, but once they were in the coffins, he did an awful thing. He just nailed the lids shut. If you listen, you can hear them scratching from the insides." Dunbar left the girls in the chapel. She hooked the door latch so they couldn't leave. They had one candle between them that eventually went out. Dunbar was right. They could hear the scratching.

Cleaning

Azalea began waking Aza in the middle the night. She would make her perform chores. While Aza did so, Azalea would pinch her and pull her hair. In the morning, the girls knew Azalea was awake by the sound of ice cubes clanking in a crystal tumbler.

Nickname

Micajah turned the front parlor into his bedroom. If you went to see him, that is where you did your visiting. One morning Ginger went to visit. He had a nickname for Ginger. He said, "Tricky, come on in here." She entered the room and saw her grandfather's fat naked body. He had one leg propped on a chair and he was masturbating. He said, "Tricky, have a seat." Ginger ran out of the house. She didn't know what to do. If she ran along the main road, he could drive up and she knew he carried a shotgun in the truck, but if she went through the woods he could find her because he knew every inch of them from hunting. She chose the woods. When she made it home, she vomited on the porch steps. Azalea said, "Jesus Ginger, you look like hell. Why don't you go take a bath." Later, Micajah came for dinner. Ginger asked to be excused early. As she was leaving the table, he said, "Your momma sure does make a mean pork chop, Tricky."

The South Pacific

Azalea and Willie's nephew, Stiney, returned from the South Pacific and was not the same. The general consensus was he had "seen something" which had the unfortunate effect of turning him into a homosexual. The three were drinking when Willie told Stiney that Azalea would make a man of him. At Willie's insistence, Azalea and Stiney went into the bedroom and began to have sex. Then Willie got mad and grabbed an axe. Faryn, Aza, Ginger, and Trulie found their father chopping down his bedroom door. Through the cinders, they could see Azalea sitting on top of cousin Stiney. Willie entered the room with the axe. The girls urged Azalea to take their hands and run. They ran into the woods where they hid. It was winter and Azalea was naked. They made plans all night. One of the girls would sneak into the house and grab a dress for Azalea. After Azalea had clothes on, they would run until they got to town where they would buy a house and live. When the sun was rising, Azalea said, "Time to go home." They questioned her about the plan. Azalea said they would finish talking about it later. When they returned to the house, Stiney was gone and Willie was passed out on the porch holding an axe in one hand and an empty tumbler in the other with his zipper undone.

 *Dates*

The girls begged permission to have dates, but Willie refused. Finally, one of the girls figured out how they could have dates. The young man would arrive unannounced an hour before the date was to officially begin. He would walk up to the house and greet Willie holding a fifth, telling him whose son he was. Willie would then inquire about the young man's family and suggest having a drink to toast the happy coincidental meeting. An hour after the respective date and Willie had been drinking on the front porch, the girls would come out, dressed and ready. Willie could never refuse the young man an evening out with his daughters after such delightful conversation. Willie kept the fifth. The young man drove the girls to designated meeting places where the rest of the dates were waiting, and the night resumed.

Bracelets

Aza slit her wrists. Her gashes were not bad enough to kill her. The doctor did not do a good job sewing her up, so she was left with permanent scar bracelets. Azalea did not visit her in the hospital. Willie did once. He said, "Do you know what this could have done to your mother?" After spending a week in the hospital, Aza returned home. Azalea and Willie were drunk. Aza went into the kitchen. Trulie was seated at the table, eating a bowl of cereal. There was a bottle of whiskey on the counter. Aza smiled, lifted it to her mouth and looked at her sister.

⟋ *Plumbing*

Dunbar's husband Haggard abhorred indoor plumbing and wearing clothes while sleeping. During one of the worst winters on record, he woke up and let himself outside to take a piss off the front porch. While doing so, the door closed. When he tried to reenter the house, it was locked. He did not think to break a window. The following evening, Dunbar came outside for the first time since the previous day and saw him sitting in the front yard, dead. She fixed a drink and went to Azalea and Willic's.

Texas

Faryn completed her two-year fashion design college course in Kansas. She had no way to return to Mississippi. Micajah paid for Stiney, Aza, Ginger, and Trulie to drive to Kansas, attend the graduation ceremony, and bring Faryn home. Stiney insisted on taking, what he called, the creative route. At a rural truck stop cafe in Texas, he presented Faryn with a graduation present. He said, "Faryn, I've always just been goddamned crazy about you. This gift is one of a practical nature. Never take any shit from a man." The gift was a lady revolver with a mother-of-pearl handle. She put it in her handbag. That summer Trulie and Aza fell in love with a cousin whom they both promptly lost their virginity to. Ginger got completely naked in a bed with a boy but did not have sex with him.

Tennessee

Aza's respectable boyfriend asked her to marry him. Meanwhile, Andy Fox drove a convertible Cadillac into town. No one knew who Andy Fox was, but he seemed rich. He drank bourbon from a monogrammed silver flask. When Aza's fiancé came down with the flu, she went on a date with Andy Fox. He took her to a juke called The Magic. After paying the door cover, you could drink all the whiskey you wanted. Aza had her share. Later, the police raided The Magic. An officer recognizing Aza told her if she left at once he would not tell her father. Back in Andy Fox's convertible, Aza said, "You goddamned boy, why don't you give me one of those fancy cigarettes." Andy Fox said, "If you were my wife you wouldn't be using language like that." Aza said, "Well, I'm not your wife." Andy Fox drove to Tennessee. First thing in the morning, the two were legally married. Andy Fox rented a cheap motel room. The last thing Aza remembered was her head hitting the headboard which shook the attached shelf causing a Vaseline jar to fall.

Cornfield

Willie was driving home after court, when to his left in the middle of a decaying cornfield, he saw Death. He looked exactly the same as the last time he had seen him. When Willie got home, he made a drink and told Azalea he had seen Death again.

Old Highway 61

Azalea, Willie, and the girls went to town to go Christmas shopping. When they got home, they heard Dunbar's laughter. They assumed she was in the kitchen, making a drink. Willie shouted hello but Dunbar did not answer. Walking by the corridor sideboard, Azalea noticed a drawer open. She saw that the only contents was the previous year's Christmas card from Dunbar. The telephone rang. Willie answered it. His face fell and he hung up the phone. He told the family that three hours earlier, Dunbar and Haggard, Jr. had been in a car accident on old Highway 61. Both perished. Dunbar was killed by decapitation.

Hitchhiker

Willie picked up a vagrant hitchhiker and brought him home. He told Azalea to go in the bedroom and have sex with the vagrant hitchhiker. Azalea became angry. A fight broke out. The vagrant hitchhiker became afraid and ran away.

MOTHERHOOD OBJECTS

Lives of the Saints

Pet Rabbit

Instructions

Pet Chicken

Japonica Bluff

Vitamins

Southern Lifestyles

Lines

Willie and Azalea were broke. They began to lag on their loan payments to Micajah. Despite that they had almost paid off Mary's Down, Micajah had them evicted. They lost the house and everything in it. Willie had a heart attack, then open-heart surgery. During the surgery there was a complication. Willie said he left his body and floated into a tunnel of light. A voice told him it was not his time and he was sucked back into his body. Ginger converted to Catholicism. Stiney began sending Trulie death threats and love letters. The letters became more detailed and he was institutionalized in the state asylum, then released. Toomsata burned to the ground. No identifiable cause was found. Azalea drank herself into a coma, but pulled through. Micajah died. At the reading of the will, the executor read, "I leave Azalea not a god-damned thing."

Pet Rabbit

Aza and Andy moved into a garage apartment. Aza became sick. After several weeks, she went to the doctor. She thought she had the flu, but was pregnant. The couple did not get along. Aza moved back in with Willie and Azalea. They said Aza and Andy should reconcile because they were going to have a child. Andy gave Aza a pet rabbit for a reconciliation gift and she moved back into the garage apartment. Aza named the pet rabbit Eleanor. One afternoon Aza returned to the apartment and noticed Eleanor was not in her cage. Shirtless, Andy was sitting in front of the TV starting on his third six-pack, eating cooked rabbit. It turned out he wanted to marry Aza because he, mistakenly, thought her father was rich.

Faryn married her high school sweetheart. Ginger went to college, joined a sorority, and announced her engagement to a promising accounting student, a short, hot-tempered Russian Jew. Trulie kept busy sewing her own wedding dress. Aza filed for divorce and moved back in with Willie and Azalea. She never saw Andy Fox again.

Instructions

The night before Trulie's wedding, Stiney came to the house. Azalea, Willie, and Stiney were drinking. Trulie was busy putting last-minute details in order for the wedding. Later, Stiney followed Trulie down the corridor. He grabbed her wrists and pinned her against the wall and said, "I'm going to follow God's instructions and rape you." Trulie struggled free after kicking Stiney in the balls. Azalea and Willie remained drunk throughout Trulie's wedding ceremony.

Pet Chicken

Aza delivered a girl. She named her Penelope, which was not a family name. Aza rented a basement apartment in town for herself and the baby. After a weekend visit, toddler Penelope said she wanted to stay with Willie and Azalea. Azalea was hospitalized again for drinking herself into undulations. It was agreed that she would trade in drinking for raising Penelope. Azalea and Willie bought Penelope a pet chicken and Willie painted a portrait of Penelope and the chicken.

Japonica Bluff

With little money, Willie moved Azalea and Penelope to Japonica Bluff. Japonica Bluff was a dilapidated antebellum farmhouse. It did not have a proper address. It was past where Churchyard Road ended, through Goat Alley, and on the edge of the Devil's Punchbowl.

Churchyard Road was named for the antebellum cemetery that lined the unpaved road. Past the cemetery, the road narrowed, eventually turning into Goat Alley, a community of poor blacks who lived in shotgun shacks. It was called Goat Alley because there were an unusual number of goats and they did not have strings tied around their tails. Goats' tails are tied so they will fall off. In the country, a goat with a tail is considered spiritually unclean. When you encounter a goat, you look at its ass. If it has a tail, you invoke the name of Jesus and leave the site at once.

Japonica Bluff was on the edge of the Devil's Punchbowl. The Devil's Punchbowl was a dense bayou. You could not see the bottom of the Devil's Punchbowl and you could not see across it. On the other side that you could not see was the Old Beau Repose Trace. The Trace was one of the oldest roads in the United States, and was the first road in the Mississippi Territory. Before the u.s. government claimed it, it was an Indian footpath. Before that, it was an animal path.

Two brothers built Japonica Bluff in the early 1800s. Pretending to be travelers, the brothers would befriend lone travelers on the Old Beau Repose Trace. The brothers would spend two nights with the traveler. They would eat with him, sing campfire songs with him, and the three would share counsel concerning issues of the day. On the third night the brothers would murder the traveler. They would enter the Devil's Punchbowl with the corpse and resurface on the other side at the family home, Japonica Bluff. Once there, they would chop the victim into pieces and eat him. They always kept the head intact by sticking it on the end of a wooden pole. Eventually, a small mob hung the brothers at Japonica Bluff. Later, a well was dug underneath the place where the poles had been. It provided the water for the house.

~ Vitamins

Aza swallowed an entire bottle of Vitamin B pills in a suicide attempt. Everyone found it amusing, even Aza. Three weeks later she went to a bridge, partially undressed, climbed over the railing, and got her toes close to the edge. The police were called. Aza was removed from the bridge. A doctor told Aza she was going to a place where she could rest. She was sent to a private psychiatric ward where she remained for six months.

Southern Lifestyles

A southern lifestyles magazine did a feature on Willie and family. The photographs show him smoking a pipe in a garden and Azalea and Aza playing chess in the parlor. Aza frowns in the picture. Her posture is poor. Later she says this is because her hair was damp and it depressed her to have her photograph taken while having damp hair.

Lines

Aza began dating an electrical engineer. His mother disliked Aza because she was trouble. The couple eloped. When Aza's new husband phoned to tell his mother, she was entertaining the local mortician and his wife. She said, "Everything is lined up, they can bury me now." Faryn, Aza, Ginger, and Trulie all became pregnant. Nine months later, they each delivered a baby within a week of one another. Faryn begot Abella, Ginger begot Mary, Trulie begot Alea, and Aza begot me.

P S A L T E R : (Birth Interim)

iii

"*Those songs could be heard
in the ears of dogs*"

Vein-laden tracks gather, thighfat the *click click* sound. I knit. Wasp nest stitch. We are weighted. Red eclipsed meat shaded. Found bones inter frozen ground. Our shelves are thin, our sugars, hard. We winter amid the lining.

Easter makes them we make them
we eat we eat eat them. A hard
boiled trick egg comes out her
palm. Her blood hand holds her
white hand.

*T*AKE CARE OF ME SAVIOR to not wake them, to walk among them. I will put on the black wool mittens, Savior. To protect from habits, these dark, Christless days. To shuck our lot of corn, Lord. To rise early and never complain. To redeliver false baby, Savior. The nurse jammed me with a finger, Sweet Jesus, she wore a white latex glove. My name written in Psalms, to recite, Savior, to recite my name written in the Psalms. To pray on my knees for the eternal soul of her, my mother, Christ, my sucked, and I, absences of mother, Christ. To tell, Savior, of the cut cut incottoned stain. To red the paddle of flower, Lord, where labia agaped to center the bone, Lord. Shiny purse and funerals, Savior, to never complain of swollen issues, corn shuckings, and such. To will for it is best not to be, Savior, to not be *sweetheart* again. These are dark, Christless days, Savior, take care of me.

You will expel a seed. Bitch hip dripping operating theater table edge. Girl Confederates, ride out to war. Oxidize Stirrup Bridge with hotlamp vaginal curdle smell. Jowl quiver overhang. Wrap it round. Glove will snatch corner air laid into iodine tile. Fleshpink powder-sucked, he shall pop the milky glove. Rifling through pockets of bloody Rebs, you are women now.

Welld   I   wish   I   was   in   de   land   ob   cotton
old   times   dere   am   not   forgotten
look   away   look   away   look   away
Dixie   land   in   Dixie   land
whar   I   was   born   in   early   on   one   frosty
mornin'   look   away   look   away
look   away   Dixie   land
to   live   and   die   in   Dixie   in   Dixie   in   Dixie
men   take   their   stand   in   Dixie   land
so   we   can   die
in Dixie.

iv

"As a result of the occupation,
letters were passed
in the margins of books"

Repetition ———

My grandfather sat in a leather armchair for the second half of his life. He did not sleep in bed. During day, he might lie down for an hour or he might take naps sitting in his chair. He told stories. Family stories, moral stories, the story about the time he saw Jesus, and personal adventure stories. I would sit in a rocking chair in front of his leather chair and listen. When he repeated himself I thought it was because he was trying to reinforce the stories because he would say over and over the most important thing was to know one's history. Sometimes I thought he had a bad memory. He told every story, no matter how many times he had told it, like he was telling it for the first time. I listened to every story, no matter how many times I had heard it, like I was hearing it for the first time. We called my grandfather Lally. Whenever my mother, one of her sisters, or my grandmother referred to him in front of children, they said, "Your Lally." It was understood. He was extraordinary so he did not have to be like other husbands, fathers, grandfathers. He could live in a chair.

He knew my name. Sometimes he said it when he wanted me to get him coffee, which he drank all day and night, sometimes when he wanted me to rub his legs. He sat in the duct-taped chair and ached. I would rub my hands up and down his placid calves, hard and fast. Large patches of yellow dead skin flaked into the air and I could not look. He told the same stories over and over. I listened to everything he said. Sometimes it was excruciating.

yellow vitamin pills yellow vitamin pills iron claw-foot bathtub water iron claw-foot bathtub water a paring knife a paring knife thirteen bottles of liquor thirteen bottles of liquor a .44 a .44 requested strangulation requested strangulation pyre on fire pyre on fire starvation starvation self willed car accident with small child self willed car accident with small child jumping jumping tumor tumor vomit (possibly accidental) vomit (possibly accidental) severe electrolyte imbalance severe electrolyte imbalance in a swamp, alone in a swamp, alone an insane husband an insane husband an insane husband an insane husband splay ladder. A manicured menstrual cotton square, broken shells, a gray hair. I'm too exhausted to kill myself tonight, Dear, so just hush.

Repetition ———

Her mother's car is a Beetle-bug color of insect wings. In the back of the Beetle-bug is a rounded space carpeted with beige fuzz. Stuck into the beige fuzz is red lollypop glue merged with broken plastic cup piece. If she wants, she can kneel back there but she likes it in the front. After work her mother picks her up from daycare and she stands in the front seat while her mother drives.

Her head doesn't touch the roof. There are pin-sized brown dots on the white canvas of the roof. There are knobs like rolly-pollies for the radio. On the seat by her feet, there are rips in the vinyl. Orange disintegrating foam squeezes out of the rips. The edges of the vinyl are like knives that cut the foam. Sometimes she gets a favorite treat when she gets in the car. Pastel powdered sugar that matches the color of the plastic container it comes in. The purple plastic container has light purple sugar. The green plastic container has light green sugar. Sometimes the powdered sugar just comes in a square paper straw. The paper straw gets soggy from slobber. Then she can taste the paper. She hates the taste of paper. She rides standing up. It is her special way of riding.

The road is long, flat, gray, and wide. The little girl sings The Itsy Bitsy Spider loud. It is raining. The Beetle-bug rattles and chugs down the road. It is hot. The little girl's hair sticks to her forehead. She watches the rain fat plopping tears on the window.

There is a ditch on the side of the road. The woman drives with both hands clutching the steering wheel. The ditch is like a river. Standing on her seat, the little girl can see it. The woman says, See that ditch. It is the ditch like a river. I could just drive into that ditch, the woman says. She jerks the steering wheel hard and the little girl goes forward. There is a clink when head and tooth hit glass. She gets back on the seat, but sits.

The little girl looks at the ditch speeding by. The woman is smiling. I could just drive right into that ditch she says. There is a paper bag between her legs and a wet spot on the woman's thigh where the fabric is pulled tight. She takes the Budweiser can out of the paper bag and says, Get me another one. There are some beneath the little girl's feet on the floorboard of the Beetle-bug.

The little girl likes the way it smells down there. You can hear what the road sounds like down there. She puts her hands around the hot can and gives it to her mother who puts it between her legs. The woman swerves the car toward the ditch, then pulls it back straight. The woman swerves the car toward the ditch, then pulls it back straight. The woman swerves the car toward the ditch, then pulls it back straight. The woman swerves the car toward the ditch, then pulls it back straight.

The Place Where One Wrote ⟶

Few memories, those years. One is seeing wood floor from the iron bed. I am told it was before I fell and "broke my head open." One is seeing a person in a wheelchair at the grocery store. The person in the wheelchair's leg had been amputated. The amputated leg was not covered. The leg looked severed, but clean. It was surrounded by thick red. Not red like meat, red like purpled beet gelatin. The person was not wearing any clothes. The wheelchair was rusted and broken. As I sat in my mother's cart and we rolled by, the person's head turned and watched us leave the store.

The memory that is clear I remember doing only once, but in the memory I remember I had done it before and that I would do it again. I know because in the memory, I went to the yellow desk with a feeling. I had a bedroom and beside my bed was an old yellow desk. In the center of the place where one wrote, a red flower had been painted.

Standing in front of the desk, I could not see the red flower. I pulled myself up. I was aware I might hurt myself.

I drug my face over the desktop. My chin skipped, making a squeal. My weight was less than that of the desk because I did not tip it over. It never moved. My upper body was on the desktop and my legs stuck straight out in the air.

I positioned myself so that the red flower was between my legs. Holding on to the sides of the desktop, I pressed my pubic bone down until the desired feeling was created then I released myself from the desk, trying to be careful, but falling and biting my tongue. There was blood in my mouth. I remember an olive slant.

Eraser ⟶

She found it in the corner. She picked it up. Brought it close. This happened at a time when her head was unusually large. She loved games. Two favorites being "Cleaning Out Shoes" and "Feeling Old People's Skin." In "Cleaning Out Shoes" she would take a bobby pin and run it through the grooves on the bottoms of people's shoes, removing and examining minute grit, color of raisins. In "Feeling Old People's Skin" she would move her hand down the arms of old people with her eyes closed. These were not the same as finding something. She found an eraser. In the corner, a pink beat-up novelty eraser in the shape of a robot based on a cartoon character called "Transformer." The eraser had been used. She held it between two gummy fingers in front of her large head.

She could see the gray sheen of sensitive recollected pencil in buffered streaks. The robot eraser had many details, just like a real robot would have had. It had robot-style legs and feet and arms and hands. Its head was a robotic nub. Robots had small heads. She found that if she took her finger and gently rubbed the soft gray and used areas, she could remove the pencil from the eraser so that her fingerprints absorbed the shiny graphite. She found this action had the effect of polishing the robot eraser. Shortly thereafter, she decided the eraser was God. After, there was no questioning the divine status of the eraser. She put Him in her pocket and returned to her desk. Everything had changed but at the same time, not.

The eraser was God which meant it was no longer an eraser. She told herself that she did not want to take God's body with a firm grip and move Him back and forth so that He heated up and created eraser curlicues and sometimes a horrible, dreadful, appalling noise as He was rubbed across another texture so contrary to His own nature. No one ever saw God. She was careful with Him but it seemed remarkable that no one happened to look up and see what they would have perceived to be an eraser. Every day she polished Him with her fingertips. God was achieving a high buff.

She would take God out of her pocket during class in intervals and look at Him. She would also allow herself this privilege when recess began and before it ended. She would go to the bathroom, enter a stall, close the stall's door, slide the lock in place, take Him out of her pocket, and look at Him.

The longer she was the custodian to God, the more she became aware of his nuances, the robot shapes that formed His little robot body. She began to develop a heightened sensibility about the preciousness of God. He required a particular maintenance. This is why He could not be used in a typical eraser fashion. The enemy of God was paper and looking at God she knew where the vulnerable areas were. God's head was such an area.

She told herself to leave God's head alone, but she could not help examining it. The head had suffered a slight severing from the body. A clean incision about halfway through the neck, so if one were not careful it would be easy to remove the head completely. There were various phases with God, and this was the "playing with God's head phase."

After His vulnerability exceeded a certain risk level, she could think of nothing else. She wished to be done with her class subjects so she could pull Him out of her pocket and finger His robot head. She would insert her fingertip into the side of the pith that bore the incision and raise the nub slightly. When she did this she could briefly see the inside of God which was pink, much more pink than the outside, and not smooth, but nettled. There was a comforting sensation that accompanied lifting up God's head.

Like letting cool air into a steaming wound, and there was a wholesome clop sound when the head would again land in its proper place. These actions with their comforting sensations were followed by feelings of guilt.

After days of head aggravation, she had gone too far. It was the likely conclusion based on her patterns of behavior. God's head was hanging by a thread. It was a matter of time or of timing. The important thing was to be present when it happened. After three more days passed it rained, and when it rained the children had recess in the back of the classroom. She did not get up from her desk with the other children at recess time.

She took God out of her pocket. She looked at Him in the palm of her hand. It was going to come off. She knew this. The best thing to do was to put His head in her mouth and eat it. She placed God's head in her mouth.

God's head snapped quick. It surprised her. Bearing down on the head with the enamel of her teeth unexpectedly bloated the moment into an ecstatic loose-fitting density. He instantaneously made her tongue go dry, sucking the moisture from the inner sanctum of her mouth. As her teeth initially tested the outer skein of God, there was a subtle bounce. Grinding His head gave way to the grainy innards, like small insubstantial pearls sliding down her throat. She could taste the bitter fingerprints.

She looked at the decapitated body of God. It was ugly. She got up from her desk and walked to the back of the classroom where she originally found God. She kneeled and placed the decapitated robot eraser of God's body in the corner. She stood up and turned around. She entered the crowd of noisy children and pretended to play.

Erasing

Cousin Ruth was beautiful. She did not look like a real child. She was older, but smaller. Her skin was tight around muscles. Ruth always wanted to play the make-out game. We played the make-out game until we were twelve. After we turned thirteen, Ruth only wanted to play with boy cousins. A lot of girls wanted to play that game. I only liked it when it wasn't playing. I never wanted to play the make-out game with Ruth, but she was forceful. Ruth had rules.

She would take a piece of white unmarked paper. It had to be that kind of paper. She would begin folding the paper back and forth, over and over, until she could make a clean tear. If it was a fragmented tear she would start over. After she tore the paper in half, she would fold half of one of the halves so many times the paper almost fell apart. She would repeat this process until she was left with a small rectangular piece of paper that fit across her lips. It had to be enough to cover her lips, absolutely no lip could be showing, but it could not be excessive, there could not be any extra paper covering flesh. If it was not exact, she would get a new piece of paper and begin again.

She would press the paper across her lips. It would fall off the first few times she did this, then it would stick just enough. She would pull my head to hers with both hands. She held my head hard so that I could not move it. She would mash our lips together, close her eyes, and move her head back and forth. I never closed my eyes. Her cheeks would streak red. She had a stupid look on her face.

Ruth got sloppy. I could feel the paper change from dry, to moist, to warm soaking. I hated the taste of her insides. Thick saliva infested with sweet heat. I hated the texture of erasing paper by saturation. Images of rotten pancakes floating in water. At a certain point, my body would convulse. Ruth would gather her lips around her teeth so that her lips were hard. She would push the paper with her bone mouth into my swollen lips until they were forced to part. The game ended when I ate the paper. She would not stop until I swallowed it. That was the rule.

White Erases Red ~

The telephone was a black relic reserved for the long corridor. I remember it ringing twice. Once it was an aunt calling from Lake St. John to tell my grandmother she was having another baby. The other time it was my uncle who lived in town. He was calling to speak with my grandfather. My grandfather did not talk on the telephone so it was exciting. After, my grandfather walked back into the room and said, "He's coming out tomorrow so we can shoot the dog." We were eating dinner.

We had two dogs, Buck and Tula. Buck was a brown Doberman pinscher and Tula was a black German shepherd. Two days earlier, my grandmother was carrying groceries up the hill to the house when she saw Tula. Tula was sitting at the top of the hill, blocking the path, watching her. When she was several feet away from him she said, move it goddamn it. Tula slowly took several steps backwards, then reared up and went for her throat. She dropped the groceries. He didn't bite her, but she said his eyes were yellow. She said he hated her, he wanted to kill her, and she knew it. It infuriated her.

The morning after Tula tried to kill my grandmother, my grandfather was on the back porch kneeling down, looking into a puddle of dog urine. In the urine there was a pink swirl and a soft tuft of hair. My grandfather lit a cigarette and looked at me. He said, "Drank some bad water." In the country this means blood has gone rotten. I looked into the urine. My sister and I were told not to leave the house that day.

The night my uncle telephoned we were eating dinner in the living room. My sister and I had TV show-themed dinner trays. Clink of silver and iron fan on the floor, moving dust. My grandmother said Tula had to die because he was rabid and he would die tomorrow. I cry-choked on the corned beef hash.

The next morning the sun hung its neck over the house, heating us red, for hours. In the afternoon I heard my uncle's truck on the gravel. He was my happy uncle who claimed to have eyes in the back of his head, but he was not happy then which made it embarrassing to see him. He was carrying emptied burlap pecan sacks. The burlap sacks were corpse sacks and I could never think of him the same again. My grandfather was waiting on the porch steps with a shotgun. He told me to go inside the house.

I did not know where to go inside the house. My sister took off running. I yelled for her to wait, but she did not. I went to the bathroom and closed the door. The bathroom and everything in it was white. A white iron bathtub. White linoleum tiles on the floor. White ivory soap smelling lung bleach white. I got on my knees and put my hands over my ears. I would take my hands away from my ears and listen to the nothing, then slap them back. I could hear the nothing through the slap. I finally heard the shotgun blast. My hands were away from my ears. There was a line, a chord. It began at my vagina and ended at my mouth. It kept my insides together. The shotgun blast sprung me.

Early House

"don't touch it"; backyard apple tree groundshades the thrown and wasted doll; we walk on wood floors; the parental bedspread is patterned paisley mold purring; for the eviscerated disappearing waking times; of much later; we have a family; room with a red carpet of individuated strands; limp spider legs pinned to a stapled-down gut; once a mushroom grew from the damp corner; we discover it en route to see *The Ten Commandments;* we must take a photo; I pose by the mushroom; with a charming look on my face; while we are gone the black cat eats it; like we knew she would; Christ nothing; good ever lasts; marcate time; with lines of asylum; behind the line; lining it up; of marigolds and of asters; a girl there busted; an overcast day; blood did trickle in little bits; white bread poolside lunches; waiting; to get back in again; what's the word; Corn Whiskey Thunderbird; what's the price; one dollar twice; I met Satan; he was clear; between air and music; the music was a bad Hall & Oates song; the air was menthol cigarette smoke; Mother pretended to be dead; on the couch and was; sex pumped by an overweight man; cremated Great Grandmother sent a present; a black bent pipe cleaner; with a black bean face; playing a bottle cap banjo; sitting on a miniature bale of cotton; the priest visited; said; last time he picked me up, I hurt his back; house interior; linoleum; aluminum seared; the insides of cans and brains; the doorknobs have been removed; we are in the house; it is night; rolls of butcher paper; lying still; we trace one another; we do this from our hiding place; we are playing Sardines; the last one to find us will come into this darkness; and we shall shout; SAR-DINES; touch it; some solar tender through the small metal holes; in the front yard; I turned; saw; my house; was every color

House With A Red Door ⟶

Outside there was a garden, a swimming pool, and an overgrown lot. On the lot there was a house and swimming pool like our house and swimming pool except the house had been destroyed so only the steps that led to nowhere remained and the swimming pool was filled with black water.

After we moved in the first thing my mother did was to have our swimming pool painted blue. It took days. After it was painted and dry, she looked into the empty deep end, her toes curled around the hot edge. She was holding a garden hose. Between her legs, tubing color of grasshoppers. She lifted her arm in front of her and held the narrow hose in her fist, then let it go. She stood there looking into the deep end.

I had two inner tubes. One, from a garage sale, was oversized with wide pastel stripes. It was as tall as I was which meant it could be used for trick purposes, not utilitarian ones. The other was from TG&Y. It cinched around the waist. It was supposed to be a duck. You could smell the plastic of it.

Once my mother was going to a cocktail party at sunset. My friend Carla was to baby-sit. Carla was five years older than me which made her ten. Carla and I were swimming. I had the duck on. I could hear my mother approaching the swimming pool to say good-bye, but before I could see her, I slipped out of the inner tube. I was in the deep end. I sank. Things slowed, were blue and pleasant. Then there was a terrible hugging. But after, things became clear. I liked it.

Without warning, my mother ruptured the hush. In her beaded gown, she dove in and pushed me through the surface of water. In her slippery grasping, she scratched me. There was a silver silk cord suspended from her wrist. Around us, strands of sequins. Loose fin glove of blue floaters. The sky was pink. We were facing each another and she was holding me.

She didn't go to the cocktail party because after that she was ruined. When Carla's father, "Uncle Stew," found out Carla didn't save me, he yelled at her because she was old enough to save me, but didn't. My mother eventually became angry with me. She hated saving children.

Chapel Feed ⟶

After work, my father would drive us to the grocery
store. We would go to the deli and a used-up woman
with blue veined hands would put our selections in sty-
rofoam containers. Macaroni and cheese drenched
greens white roll fried potatoes pink jam marshmallow
paste smeared yellow cake. Once my father hired the
widow across the street to make us casseroles, but we
did not like eggplant. We returned to drive-thrus. The
day-long attempt to quit drive-thrus and the inability to
do so. My father took a cooking class. He made a mushroom dip, color of fatigues that tasted of onions.

When I was seven I went to visit my mother. She was just
out of a treatment center, living in an apartment on St.
Clare Avenue. The first night she warmed up a can of
SpaghettiOs. While I was eating, she gave me a book of
antebellum-themed paper dolls because she said I loved
them. She wasn't eating. I was aware of each bite I took.
The metal clack of the spoon. When I was halfway
through, she said, "SpaghettiOs are your favorite."

When I lived with her as a teenager, I ate mostly
SpaghettiOs and thirty-five-cent bear claws. I would

put a lot of cheese on top of the SpaghettiOs. Cheap sweet sauce and microwaved yellow clumps in a tin water orange. Over time it became harder to eat the SpaghettiOs so I added more cheese to try and get them down.

When I came home from college for a visit, my mother made a grilled cheese sandwich for me. The bread was oversaturated with grease and the sandwich fell apart on the aqua plate. I couldn't eat it, but I couldn't tell her why.

Growing up, sometimes I would stay at my grandmother's house when things at my mother's house were especially bad. Once she said no. She said no like she was taking a stand. My grandmother knew it was a violent life. When I asked if I could stay, she never asked why. Though it was never explained, I always believed she said no because when I stayed at her house, I ate too much food.

The year my grandmother died, I was obsessed with Christmas. I started shopping in August. By early October, I had expensive gifts for everyone except her. Each night when I would take the gifts out of the closet, spread them on the bed, hold them, and repackage them in their tissues, I knew her gift was absent. She died on Halloween. That year no one could appreciate their

Christmas gifts. They were too drunk and depressed because my grandmother was dead.

If there is forewarning, it is a sign by food. Food I prepare with my hands begins to taste wrong. It can be a regular day, then blotted. I feel I must eat the food fast, just as fast as I breathe, in order to avoid choking. I cannot sit while eating in this way. I begin to feel nauseous. I am aware the reasons might be because I am eating fast or maybe because the food is wrong, but I cannot untangle these reasons and I panic. I put as much of the food in my mouth as I can and try not to chew it, but swallow it dry and whole. This makes me sick.

Food becomes sublime. It geometrically squares into its complex statistics. This happens in proportion to my growing hunger. The more hungry I become, the more what food looks like and what one does with it becomes alien. Until food is pure object and all eating is apocalyptic Eucharistic. At this point, I know I am hungry, but I cannot remember what one does to alleviate hunger so I put my fingers in my mouth.

Food begins again improperly. I will eat sixteen chewable calcium supplements for a day's eating. I still cannot drink anything. I experience cramping and I vomit what food I have eaten. I bleed from ass and hands. I go to bed often, try and think about making love, but can't. I sweat through it.

Food is what you put in your mouth. You put it in your mouth. The rubber slide hidden in glossy food. And God is food. Red velvet cakes stacked in a corner of a decaying house. Pork, too. Which is fatbread saturated with rancid.

The first time was during the summer I was twelve. I put my fingers in my mouth and bit them until they bled. I was sitting on my mother's bed in the back of her new husband's trailer. I had never felt such relief. It was a cool passing through July's hanging heat.

3 a.m. Sentences On Desire —

ONE— A hunger I caught and wanted to be the object of reminds me of other times, of corn, that year I wrote myself out of marriage into ages that never were, even then I was alone a woman singing in mead halls, a red woman to give me back my him to eat corn for centuries through the death of this life I lie through the corn for another lifetime of marriages.

TWO— Appealed to me to my unresolveds, perhaps what I am looking for when I walk the catacombs, to meet the phantom film of my body which is red after time has stopped because of starvation to meet myself in the grave row, to walk into it and think it you for you to be me to never learn the difference between death and desire to learn the difference from death which cannot be extracted from the walking through.

THREE— I grew corn on a deserted island to make signals to signal to you the truth of beautiful poverty to make signals not to tell the truth through truth poverty is not beautiful to recall the red and white, the steelgun soft pierce fur plate bone smell of you, the bless thee, the keep thee, the corn apocalypse bedblood thee.

FOUR— That night your hair was iridescent cornrows and you were hungry.

FIVE— I separate the object from its consciousness so don't look at me that way.

Bone Of My ⟶

his great grandmother's pelvic set on the historic bed;
glass plate memory; between us; insurance; ligamental; a
popsuck seal; those generations; they could not have done
better; "themselves"; there is a line; of people; is it
enough; to be just this; we are always; finding ourselves;
a body; across asphalt; to wake; in parts; the sun; the sky;
subsist, continue; please do not; resuscitate; married; in a
downpour; by carved wood birds; while I slept you
watched documentaries; on the Holocaust; on ten-year-
old Scottish heroin junkies; it's like; talking to your
mother about the virtues of stylish Catholic women; like
bleeding from the ass; another year of instant generic oat-
meal; it's like; being thirsty; the neighbor child; day in,
day out; in summer and winter; scratching and scratching

Sear, -ed ———

We peel ourselves with a noon knife. Light shines through the fallen skins. One's the pitch of shotgun black, or, the black of a dog who waits for us in a house we abandoned twenty years ago. And it is summer. My grandfather lives. From his old leather chair every day at noon, he walks down the corridor. In the kitchen he takes out his knife and, while standing, peels fruit.

During night country roaches turn the white kitchen into amber sea. The bathroom is also white. It is the place I hid when my grandfather shot my rabid black dog. How can there be a place for yellow. We would hear that shotgun again.

When my mother was a girl she swallowed a bottle of yellow vitamin pills in an attempt to kill herself. Her bladder sun sack. I have seen her use that story like a pick up line. But before, there was bathtub water, color of nothing. She is five. The silver drain is a centered mermaid shingle. She makes herself go under. This will happen again, but this time it is my sister and she is five. We could have told her that trick doesn't work.

When her body changes shape and she gets that awful haircut is the year I can really see her. It is my mother. The age I was when I moved back into her house except it was never her house, but a boyfriend's trailer on the edge of a dump. At night, roaches come.

It is hot, but I tuck the blanket tight under my body for a roach seal. The blanket is stretched like a drumhead. Now and then, a roach scurries and makes a vibration. When I wake, the covers are peeled back like fruit skins. I am the age she was when she took the sharpest knife with the thinnest blade and made incisions into her wrists. The doctor sews her wrists with linen stitches and leaves little dots above and below the lines my mother has carved. The first time I ask her where they come from, I am the age she was when she tried to jump off a bridge. What she said in reply *You know Momma and Daddy are drunk again.*

She took off her clothes and danced around a burning pyre of trash and wood, then threw herself into it. A neighbor saw this happen and said she looked like a god-damned idiot. Because she was dancing, and once on fire, really dancing. When she collapsed one eye half popped out of socket. Laughter for some dyings, like vitamin ones, but not others. Not when my grandfather put a shotgun in his mouth and pulled the trigger with his toe. When he died my mother went into her bedroom and closed the door. On her dresser she lined up twelve bottles of liquor and got in bed with the shotgun.

After he shot himself, my grandfather's face was a spangle bouquet that made grass die. What is difficult about looking at something like that is not that the mind resists fragmentation in general, but that it is confounded by textures which refuse the tensions one desires through edges. Even when they took his corpse away, his head was still there, some soaking into the ground, some in liver-colored strips and bits unable to be absorbed. It looked like the oversaturated pile of womb waste on the floor between my sister's legs after she gave birth. They could have been the same. They were not but light would not have known the difference.

Kodacolor; c. 1976

ochre; chalking line; of hips inch fat; padded; soft
whipping;   reigns;   re;   semblances;   us
from   the   one;   one   name;   the   origin
al;   no   one;   can   remember;   music;
made of closeness; of so much likeness; inside our
interior; absences we pass; ladder of name's bones

Voicebirth ——

The nurse told me it was the fourth time in twelve months they'd admitted her for a suicide attempt. She said she heard my mother had also been admitted to another hospital twice for the same reason in the last twelve months, in addition to being sent to a treatment facility, also twice, same time frame, and did I know anything about that. I told her I knew about the two treatment centers and no, I didn't know about the other two attempts, different hospital. She didn't look up from her clipboard. She left the nurse's station and I stood there. The nurse's station was in the middle of the ICU ward. Radiating out from it were rooms with glass windows so the nurses could see the patients at all times. I could see my mother. She was on life support. The day before, she had taken two hundred prescription pills, washing them down with a bottle of sherry. After, she opened the door of the one-room efficiency apartment she rented and a neighbor found her. The neighbor called an ambulance then took the cash out of my mother's purse and left.

The cardiologist was drinking a Diet Coke and eating a Ding Dong. I knew before I met him to expect the worst. He said my mother did not respond to the pain sensory test they had given her that morning, something involving a metal instrument across the sternum and a needle in the sole of the foot. Her internal organs were systematically shutting down and she could not breathe on her own. They had one more test to do to determine the extent of brain trauma, but he said, more than likely based on all other tests, she was in a vegetative state. We discussed the probability that she would die on her own during the day, but if she did not, and once the final test to determine brain trauma had come back conclusive, we needed to discuss options. One of the last times I had spoken to my mother she expressed that if anything were to happen to her, she would not want to be resuscitated. I told the cardiologist this and he agreed it was a good idea not to continue supplying life support and that we would meet after her final test results had come back from the lab. He recommended that my family begin to make funerary arrangements.

My mother's sisters came and even one of her ex-husbands. I hadn't seen my aunts in a long time. They were dressed in nice clothes. We were all wearing black. Only two people at a time could be in the room with my mother and only in short intervals, so we took turns sitting in the waiting room, drinking lots of coffee.

The next morning my mother came out of the coma. No one could believe it. The doctor said, What a miracle. As he was pulling out the pink ribbed tubing that went down her esophagus and into her lungs, my mother began moaning. I imagine it. Her esophagus expanding and contracting against the pink ribbed tubing.

When the tube was out, clear liquid spit up from her mouth, ran down her chin, and onto her chest. The moan amplified. Multiple sounds started to register simultaneously in different places within the stretch of the moan. Then, these sounds started to increase and decrease in frequency. Some dimensions of the sounds sharpened and others rounded off in flat blunts. From within the moan the sounds began to clash and tremble. The edges of the sounds tremored, stuck to the low drone of the moan. All of the sudden the hard sounds and the soft sounds projected themselves away from the moan. It was like the moan was mud and the sounds had stepped out of it. With the moan as backdrop, the sounds hovered, vibrating above my mother's lips for probably a few seconds, then the sounds folded.

The backs of the sounds collapsed. Like chicken spines breaking. In a high-pitched voice, like it had been stuffed and packed with rubber balloons, she woke speaking, saying, I can talk I can talk.

V

"*C'est la guerre*"

It was bodies, what made bodies, and what bodies made. It was illegal separation. It was back-flipping in a five-star padded room. It was the Confederate Memorial Bandstand. It was sound of birds pecking glass. You could see it if you held it open. You could drink it. It was pink.

Scene ⟶

Girl (alone) on dirt road. She walks in a tire rut gutter.
Before and behind her, equidistant nothing.

She drags a stick on the road.
Where did she come from? Where is she going?
It is one hundred ten degrees.

Gesticulations ⟶

It stopped her.

Her heels, drillborned. Into the parched, impacted earth

(counterpoint). Capillaries,

shot in the pass. Her face drain: (a valve scamper). Then,

the scene ends.

Do you think she was losing her breath or catching it?
I think she was catching it.

The coffee house of seventeenth-century England was a place of fellowship where ideas could be freely exchanged. The coffee house of 1950s America was a place of refuge and tremendous literary energy. Today, coffee house culture abounds at corner shops and online.

Coffee House Press continues these rich traditions. We envision all our authors and all our readers—be they in their living room chairs, at the beach, or in their beds—joining us around an ever-expandable table, drinking coffee and telling tales. And in the process of exchanging the stories of our many peoples and cultures, we see the American mosaic being reinvented, and reinvigorated.

We invite you to the tales told in the pages of Coffee House Press books.

FUNDER ACKNOWLEDGMENTS

Coffee House Press is an independent nonprofit literary publisher. Our books are made possible through the generous support of grants and gifts from many foundations, corporate giving programs, individuals, and through state and federal support. This project received major funding from the Jerome Foundation. Coffee House Press also received general operating support from the Minnesota State Arts Board, through an appropriation by the Minnesota State Legislature and from the National Endowment for the Arts, a federal agency. Coffee House Press also received funds from the Elmer and Eleanor Andersen Foundation; the Buuck Family Foundation; the Bush Foundation; the Grotto Foundation; the Lerner Family Foundation; the McKnight Foundation; the Outagamie Foundation; the John and Beverly Rollwagen Family Foundation; the law firm of Schwegman, Lundberg, Woessner & Kluth, P.A.; Target, Marshall Field's, and Mervyn's with support from the Target Foundation; James R. Thorpe Foundation; West Group; the Woessner Freeman Foundation; and many individual donors.

To you and our many readers across the country,
we send our thanks for your continuing support.

Good books are brewing at coffeehousepress.org